EGMONT

We bring stories to life

First published in Great Britain in 2017
by Egmont UK Limited
The Yellow Building, 1 Nicholas Road, London W11 4AN

Thomas the Tank Engine & Friends™

CREATED BY BRITT ALLCROFT

HiT entertainment

ISBN 978 1 4052 8577 3
66192/1
Printed in Italy

Written by Emily Stead. Designed by Claire Yeo.
Series designed by Martin Aggett.

FSC
MIX
Paper
FSC® C018306

*This story is about the time
I thought I could manage without
my Driver. I set off by myself
one morning, and quickly
rolled into trouble . . .*

Thomas the Tank Engine had worked on The Fat Controller's Railway for many years.

He had two carriages, Annie and Clarabel, and his very own Branch Line.

Thomas was a **Really Useful Engine**.

One day on Sodor, Thomas was busy at work. He stopped at Wellsworth Station in just the right place.

"You could almost manage without me, Thomas!" laughed his Driver.

Thomas felt proud. He didn't know that his Driver was only joking!

"I don't need a Driver any more," Thomas boasted in the Sheds that night.

"Don't be silly!" peeped Percy.

"I'd never go anywhere without my Driver," said Toby. "I'd be too **frightened**."

"Well, I'm not **scared**!" said Thomas. "You'll see."

The next morning, Thomas woke up early.

"I'll show those silly Steamies," he smiled.
"My Driver says I don't need him — I'll go out
by myself. Then I'll stop and **wheesh** to wake
them up."

Thomas rolled forwards feeling very clever.
But really he was only moving because someone
had forgotten to put on his brakes!

Thomas tried to **wheesh** but he couldn't.
He tried to stop but he couldn't. He just
kept **rolling** along!

Straight ahead was the Stationmaster's house.
The Stationmaster was inside, about to have
breakfast.

"Cinders and ashes!" cried Thomas,
and he shut his eyes.

The house **rocked**, glass **smashed**. Plaster and dust flew everywhere.

The Stationmaster was furious!

His wife was cross, too. "Look at our breakfast!" she said. "Now we will have to make some more."

Workmen came to prop up the house with strong poles. Then they laid rails through the garden.

Thomas felt **terrible**. He didn't dare say a word the whole time.

Soon, Donald and Douglas arrived.

"Don't worry, Thomas. We'll get you back on the rails," they called.

Puffing hard, they hauled Thomas to safety.

Thomas' buffers were badly bent and bits of fence were stuck to them.

The twins laughed as they steamed away.

Thomas was in disgrace. The Fat Controller came to see him. "What a lot of **trouble** you have caused!" he boomed.

"I'm sorry, Sir," said Thomas quietly.

"You must go to the Steamworks to be mended," The Fat Controller went on.

"Yes, Sir," Thomas sighed.

"Meanwhile, **Diesel** will do your work,"
The Fat Controller told Thomas.

"D-D-Diesel, Sir?" Thomas spluttered.

"Diesels stay in their Sheds until they are needed,"
The Fat Controller explained. "They never roll off
to breakfast in Stationmasters' houses."

Thomas set off to the Steamworks a **sadder** and **wiser** engine.

He had learnt two things — never to leave the Sheds without his Driver, and that breakfast was not for engines.

More about the Twins

lamp

whistle

nameplate

tender

buffer

coupling hook

Thomas' challenge to you

Look back through the pages of this book
and see if you can spot:

scarecrow

cereal

clock

workmen

The Fat Controller